## Praise for Laurent Graff's *Happy Days*

"This novel makes you happy because Graff describes with a slightly bitter but delicate touch and a wonderful remove our everyday existence, and it comes out in soft colors, making fireworks out of wet timber, and a One Thousand and One Nights out of a dimly lit room. There is a little bit of Merlin in Graff, or Mary Poppins. This novel is supercalifragilistic."
—*Marie-France*

"This ode to life is marked by a strident humor. Graff's writing has as always a gorgeous fluidity."
—*Libraire Dialogues*

"In *Happy Days* Laurent Graff reflects on some of the absurdities of our existence with great tenderness."
—*Page*

"Laurent Graff has come up with a perfect little book with an original set-up. With his sharp eye, clear style, and sour irony, Graff captures our hopes and fears, foibles and follies in simple short sentences. And he also makes us laugh, even if it's a bittersweet laugh."
—*Ouest-France*

# Happy Days

## LAURENT GRAFF
translated by Linda Coverdale

CARROLL & GRAF PUBLISHERS
NEW YORK

145 0 8402

HAPPY DAYS

Carroll & Graf Publishers
An Imprint of Avalon Publishing Group Inc.
245 West 17th Street
New York, NY 10011

We wish to express our appreciation to the French Ministry of
Culture—CNL for its assistance in the preparation of the translation

First Carroll & Graf edition 2004

Library of Congress Cataloging-in-Publication Data is available.

ISBN: 0-7867-1282-1

Printed in the United States of America
Interior design by Simon M. Sullivan
Distributed by Publishers Group West

*To my children*

. . . *one must accustom the soul to serenity, which is the contented contemplation of nothingness.*

—Roger Caillois, *Pierres réfléchies*


*I threw away that tiny thing called "me" and I became the great wide world.*

—Musô Soseki

Happy Days

*Here I am, dead and buried, as if I had really lived.*

It's a lovely autumn day. Trees are shedding their foliage on the lawn; all bundled up, residents are strolling along the asphalt paths, shuffling through clumps of dead leaves; an ambulance is pulling up to what will be the new arrival's last home; sitting next to Alzheimer, my arms stretched wide on the back of the bench, my relaxed little smile hovering like a seagull on the breeze, I breathe the fresh air of the garden and grounds of Happy Days. Passing by in slow

1

motion with a towel around his neck, Bébel takes his brief morning constitutional, looking remarkably tanned in his white jogging suit. Creaking expertly along, he goes from the Home to the entrance gate and back.

"Feeling fit today, Bébel?"

"Got to stay in shape!"

At the end of the driveway stands the Home, a huge three-storied building, recently constructed, with wooden balconies in the style of a Swiss chalet. On the ground floor, the dining hall's large sliding-glass doors and flowered drapes open onto the garden. A marble plaque at the front door announces: THE HAPPY DAYS— A PRIVATE RETIREMENT HOME. There's a parking lot for the convenience of visitors. The entire establishment gives the impression of wholesome tranquillity and efficiency.

I turn to my right, where Alzheimer seems to be staring at a point off in space, frowning with concentration.

"So, where were we, Al?"

Al doesn't react, lost in some looping thought that demands his full attention.

"Ah, yes, when I was eighteen years old!"

Suddenly intrigued, it's Al's turn to look at me.

"But where do you live?"
"I'm coming to that, Al, I'm coming to that."

At eighteen, I felt I had experienced everything that constitutes, roughly speaking, the average full life, ranging from love to work, lofty ideals to crass ambition, disappointment to boredom. I had sampled, through trial runs (puerile, of course, but meaningful), the joys and disillusionments of existence, and I felt I'd gained enough insight to see that life, in its general outlines, no longer promised me any "surprising" surprises worth waiting for. I decided to live resigned to my lot, without any fuss or expectations, and prepare myself for what was coming.

"But where do you live?"

So one fine day, off I go to the savings bank where my parents have been patiently making deposits for me ever since my birth.

"You live in a savings bank?"

I present my bankbook and identity card to the cashier and tell him that I want to withdraw my money. I'm now legally of age, so I'm within my rights. The guy checks my papers, taps away on his computer keyboard, and hands me the balance in my account with a certain professional satisfaction, plus a touch of ad hoc formality, happy to be of service to a young man setting out in life. I pocket the check and head directly to my bank to deposit it. Then I go to city hall, where I ask to see the person in charge of burial plots. Thus, at an age when most young people are buying their first cars, I had decided to purchase my grave. I wanted to mark this milestone with a tombstone.

I wind up in front of a dumbfounded clerk who can't believe her ears. She asks me how old I am, expresses fresh astonishment, tries to reason with me: "You've got other things to do, at your age! You'll have plenty of time to think about it, your whole life is ahead of you. . . . Are you ill?" No, I'm in great shape, healthy in mind and body, really, I promise her. "Are you sure you want to do this?" she insists. We start to fill out the forms; she's giving me weird looks over her glasses, clearly upset, and I'm smiling at her in a friendly way. "Would you like a family vault or an individual plot?" Now, that's a question I hadn't thought about. I would almost certainly be getting married in a few years, like everyone else, and having children, if all went well; but to go ahead and make plans for their graves. . . . After a moment's reflection, not wanting to get too far ahead of myself, I finally opt for an individual plot. "A temporary grant, or in perpetuity?" "In perpetuity." She consults a ledger, a sort of mortuary register, a big account book, and writes down a location number. I ask her if it's possible to go take a look at the actual spot, the site of my future tomb. At her wit's end, she replies with a sigh that the plots are assigned automatically, in a pre-established order, and she shows me the map of the cemetery in the ledger, pointing out the two square yards that belong to me. I sign the papers and put down a deposit; I'll pay the rest when I receive the invoice in the mail. I thank the clerk warmly, but when we shake hands, hers is limp, sad, lifeless.

She seemed completely dejected and demoralized, poor thing! My visit had really shaken her. As I was leaving her office, she called after me, "I have a son your age. . . ." I flashed her one last smile and set out for a monument company.

"But where do you live?"

I don't want to crack a bad joke, but honestly, the guy at the monument company looked more like a butcher than a stone-carver: the florid complexion of a bon vivant, shocking plumpness, and an incongruous joviality (along the lines of, "So, what can I get you?") he did try to repress. "Sir?" he says, in tones of deepest sympathy, butcher knife in hand. I explain the situation, and this shrewd businessman barely bats an eye: "You're right, it's never too early to think about such things." I tell him that I'd like to adorn my grave with a headstone as quickly as possible, to give concrete form to my project. He squints at me suspiciously: "You're not planning on. . . ." No, not at all, I have no intention of doing away with myself, wouldn't dream of it; on the contrary, I want to live to the end of my allotted days. He's reassured. "We have a few models in the showroom, and more in the catalog." I take a little tour of the shop, inspecting the different marbles and granites, running an appreciative hand over the polished surface of a slab or the curve of a stele as I go by. I want something ordinary, nothing fancy or original. A gravestone. I find one that seems suitable, stashed away in a corner of the showroom: a square monument of light gray marble, the basic model. The guy seems disappointed by my choice; he'd probably have preferred that I select a more ornate stone, to do honor to his artistry. "Fine, sir, if that's the one you want." He explains that we'll have to wait for the purchase of my plot to be officially completed before going any further. "In any case, there's no hurry, is there?" He'll take care of everything and get back to me. "Have a nice day, sir!"

And that's how, at the age of eighteen, I bought my tombstone.

"But where do you live?"

It's noon. The Happy Days bell rings in the courtyard, announcing lunchtime.

"Come on, Al, let's go eat."

I help Alzheimer stand up and we proceed to the dining hall, along with other residents moving at the same slow, measured pace I have finally learned to use so that I won't always be the first one there.


The dining hall, a large, light-filled room care-fully designed not to resemble an institutional cafeteria, is appointed with cozy yet practical amenities. The floor is tiled and easy to clean, but its checkerboard pattern is handsome and stylish, without that harsh hygienic look. Round wooden tables, placed around the room at random and not too close together, provide an atmosphere of privacy for the diners. Doped up with fertilizer, green plants in decorative cachepots add gay touches here and there. Thanks to its elegant chandeliers, the dining hall rather resembles a ballroom, which it becomes, moreover, on certain occasions. Loudspeakers discreetly integrated into the decor emit soothing mood music during meals.

I hang my jacket on a coat tree in the vestibule, among the knitted scarves and woolen hats, the rustic caps, the fur-lined coats with pockets stuffed with damp hankies, and, draped over a hat peg, Bébel's towel. To avoid any bottlenecks, the nurses have already brought down the "semi-valids," who wait crossly in their seats for the meal to begin ("Why'd they bring us down so early?"). Latecomers arrive clutching the bars of their walkers, heads nodding, slippered feet inching forward as if into a minefield. Chef is already seated, firmly anchored in his adult diaper, both fists on the table, mumbling his eternal complaints. I sit at my usual place, respecting the established pattern so as not to disrupt my table companions' routine. The dining hall gradually fills up. A grumpy hubbub invades the room, punctuated by the impatient clinking of silver-ware from residents with Parkinson's disease. The Alzheimers are still circling in confusion, looking for their seats.

Going clockwise around the table, we have Bébel, with his bronzed complexion (seventy-eight years old); Le Marec and his wife Alice, the latter freshly permanent-waved and blue-rinsed after the hairdresser's visit (eighty-two and seventy-nine); Marguerite, known behind her back as The Billion, because of her legendary fortune (eighty-six); Chef, a former cook and Greco-Roman wrestler (ninety); Jean, a smiling and reticent man, who has not gotten over the death of his wife (seventy-six); and Clarisse, who's sex-obsessed, and never misses a chance to hoist up her skirts or cop a quick feel (eighty). Obviously, I stand out a bit, at thirty-five years old. In spite of this age difference—a mere formality—I have managed without much trouble to fit in and be accepted by relying on a polite and easy-going manner, and today everyone considers me a full-fledged resident.

This required at the outset that I convince the director, M. Révelli, firstly, that I wasn't crazy ("But—you ought to go into an *asylum,* old boy!"), which was not exactly obvious, and secondly, that he should make an exception and take me on as a trial resident, on payment of a surcharge in addition to the regular fee, which detail went a long way toward overcoming his reservations. The trial period proved decisive. I showed myself to be a model resident (aside from my age): calm, unobtrusive, fit, conforming with good grace to life in the Home—in short, just like M. Révelli would have wished all his other tenants to be. And so I was taken into the fold, without my status ever being officially defined. I was allowed to remain, always with the understanding that I might be asked to leave at any time.

Upset by my presence, the staff decided from the get-go that I was cuckoo. I was a challenge to the institutional identity of Happy Days, and employee representatives voiced their concerns to the director. M. Révelli explained the special nature of the situation and asked the personnel to consider me a bit like the house fool ("Well, you know what I mean. . . ."), the unusual pet, the gardener, the village idiot, the harmless softhead ("I mean, have a little compassion!"). He reassured everyone: I was a unique case—a village can't have more than one idiot. The delegated representatives agreed to try out the arrangement, and the staff made an effort to look at me as a simpleton, a gentle jerk adopted by the Home. That's how they treated me, and I became their friend ("So, Antoine, how's it goin'?").

As for the residents, they weren't too surprised by my presence. They merely asked me a few questions about what had brought me here, and, well, if it made me happy. . . . Any visitors who noticed me assumed I was an attentive son or grandson—chasing after an inheritance, they concluded, thus betraying their own ulterior motives.

Today, a vegetable medley and rabbit with mushrooms are on the menu. The waitresses move among the tables with their cart, plonking down the plated meals left and right. Animal grunts—whether from satisfaction or disgust, who can say—greet the plats du jour. I take charge of filling my neighbors' glasses (a simple precaution) with their choice of either water or wine. Water for Bébel ("This morning, my time was twelve minutes thirty seconds!"), wine for Clarisse ("When are you going to come see me, sweetie?"). At the piano,

Richard Clayderman—the European Liberace—accompanies the clatter of clumsy forks and the gummy chewing sounds of toothless mouths. Conversations are rare, for people are busy. They dig right in, like raptors. They compare their portions to their tablemates' servings and feel cheated. They're not hungry anymore, and they leave half their food. I don't pay any attention to this circus now, I'm used to it, and eat quietly in my corner. I do not consider my companions with a critical, wickedly ironic eye. I simply witness the unbearable decline that lies in wait for us all, with the absurdity of death for a finale. I can no longer live outside of that truth.

Dessert arrives: the treat that titillates the taste buds and lights up leering eyes. Each of us selects a pastry from among the three on offer, with fruit the consolation prize for those with high cholesterol. Turning on the charm, Clarisse tries to cadge seconds from Jean, who gives in. Bébel begins to sniff dramatically all around him and glares at Chef, who looks down, ashamed, quivering with embarrassment in his chair. The waitresses follow up immediately with coffee, while some residents start returning to their rooms. It's time for a nap or a TV soap opera. At a neighboring table, an old lady wriggles in her wheelchair; she doesn't want to miss the beginning, shouts angrily for someone to come get her. The nurses chat and calmly finish their coffee; *The Young and the Restless* can wait. I stand up without a word. Clarisse gives me a wrinkly smile ("Where're you off to, honey?").

Leaning against a pillow, I'm lying on my bed watching *The Young and the Restless* on television. The room is spacious and bright, pleasantly furnished, and equipped with every modern comfort. The Happy Days is a deluxe retirement home offering medical personnel on staff, luxurious amenities, and varied activities (memory workshops, games, outings, shows). The motto here is: "Science adds years to your life; The Happy Days adds life to your years." I would have preferred someplace more ordinary, more Spartan, but I didn't find anything else within a twenty-mile range, and I wanted to keep an eye on my grave. I can afford Happy Days thanks to a providential inheritance from someone who was almost a complete stranger to me, a long-lost godfather without any other heirs, a man my parents chose (way back when) to honor a friendship they believed would prove indestructible and forever faithful. At first life simply put some distance between these friends, and then it separated them for good. This godfather became the ghost of my parents' vanished youth, until the day a notarized document arrived informing them of his death. I invested the fruits of my inheritance in a suitable account, which would finance my early retirement, according to my calculations, for a good fifty years.

Pamela is in love with her father-in-law Jack, who is torn between affection for his son Michael and indifference toward his wife Ashley, a depressed and serious alcoholic. Jack's endless shilly-shallying was always echoing through the whole house at top volume, so one fine day I decided to add the picture to the sound. Ever since, I've had to explain the different plot developments and subtleties of the scenario to any residents who can't follow the action. They question me in the lounge, in the hall, and come looking for me in my room for clarifications. Patiently, I summarize, answer questions, encouraging speculation and promoting suspense, like a real soap-opera flack. Arms and legs crossed on my bed, I follow the daily episode, taking the occasional note.

After the closing credits, still reclining, I study the ceiling. Out in the hall, the nurses make their rounds of the rooms, changing diapers and asking how everyone feels, listening to each person's litany of misery and prescribing placebos to satisfy the whiners. There's a knock on my door. Christine enters in her white smock and shuts the door behind her. Without a word, she comes over and sits on the edge of the bed. Taking my hand, she shoves it right between her thighs. I let her, playing the innocent. This little game has been going on for several months and always follows the same ritual. Next Christine unbuttons her smock, revealing two large breasts she then frees from their bra cups so that I can suck them. I do that while she unfastens my belt. She gives me a little hand job and sucks me. Then she gets up on the bed and sits astride me. She gets busy, jiggling her buttocks and doing pelvic thrusts. She turns around and I have to take her doggy-style. She moans a bit, flinging her head back and forth. I moan, too. After she's left the room, I stay stretched out on the bed and study the ceiling. I've had my placebo.

\*    \*    \*

I'm married—not for much longer, the divorce is almost official—and the father of two.

After high school, I played at being a college student. I regularly visited my headstone, which bore my name and date of birth, followed by a hyphen. I started to think about an epitaph. The first one I had engraved on a plaque (later on, I replaced it) said:

> *O you, divine nymph with the lovely ass*
> *Caress my marble as you sashay past*
> *Marvelous moons of my eternal night*
> *Where I lie I leer at your rays of light.*

I was obsessed with women. At that time, I was going to whores a lot. Not that I was incapable of scrounging up my own girl, but I couldn't be bothered to cruise for them, to look for openings and then deal with the preliminaries and chitchat. That whole complicated ritual didn't interest me in the least, when, I mean, the unspoken object is to get the girl into your bed. Plus, I was fed up with perpetual-adolescent love, I wanted to settle down as soon as possible, enough already. Always my tendency to get a head start on the inevitable.

I finally dropped out of college after two years and looked for work. Fairly quickly I found a job as a warehouse man in a delivery firm. I simply took what turned up, without checking it out too much—after all, well or badly paid, I'd still get by. I set myself up in a modest apartment in the city and began to sift through the personals, figuring that this system saved a lot of wasted words. I picked out the most candid ads, the ones with the fewest requirements and conditions. Unfortunately, most of the time I ended up with more hookers, lying in ambush. Still, I did meet a few girls who were more or less sincere and disinterested, but who would quickly have become troublesome. I wanted a simple woman, modest, docile, with whom I could serenely contemplate the future: a wife.

After a few months of fruitless searching, at last I met a girl about my age, a bit of a lost soul, quite timid, who was also looking to settle down. She believed in true love and was foolish enough to think I might be hers. I didn't contradict her, she'd see the light soon enough. Aside from that, she wasn't very demanding or complicated; it didn't take much to make her happy, as long as I assured her of my devotion. When we started living together, I must admit that I even let myself get caught up in the game, and fairly easily, too: If there was a little bit of happiness to be had before fate carried it away. . . . I remained perfectly lucid, however, and knew that love would one day turn to boredom. After a year we got married, and the next year she was carrying our first child. Now and then we visited my grave, lugging along a bucket and a gardening fork to clean the headstone and weed the plot. She'd gotten used to that, thought it a tad unusual, but allowed as how we all came to it in the end. I'll leave out the first symptoms of our predictable disintegration as a couple—the reproaches, sulks, the growing resentment. We had our second child a year after the first (quickly done is well done), before desire vanished completely and made procreation a chore: A boy and a girl, that was enough. At first I tried to take care of my children, give them the taste for life that I lacked; I probably botched it or wasn't convincing enough. When they began to grow up, they let me know that they didn't need me to formulate their personal ideas about existence. Then my wife began having notions of her own, grandiose ambitions, and dreams of a different reality. I let her dream, and reality began telling her to come home later and later in the evening. After twelve years of marriage, it looked like the end. Fate took a hand, giving things a nudge with a fortunate turn of circumstances when my unknown godfather left me his fortune. Once again, I forged ahead: I told my wife and children that I was leaving them. Tropical climes didn't tempt me; I wanted peace and quiet, far from the tedious vicissitudes of existence. I wanted to let myself drift gently on the surface of life, floating on my back until I wound up flat on my back six feet under. At thirty-five years old, I chose to live in a retirement home. And here I am, sitting next to you, Al.

"But where do you live?"

*Cradle to coffin, from one box to another.*

The sky has clouded over. A chilly wind assails the few residents trudging around the grounds, muffled in their many layers of clothing. Bébel stubbornly battles the elements to stay in shape. Sitting on my bench, I smoke a cigarette, alone. Alzheimer was taken to the hospital yesterday, the victim of a heart attack. I watched my memory leave in an ambulance.

Today, after lunch, there will be a trip to the animal park at Thoiry. The bus hired by the management for the afternoon is already waiting in the parking lot. The driver is pacing up and down in the courtyard with his hands in his pockets, stamping his feet to keep warm. He notices me and comes over for a bit of a chat.

"Cold enough for you?"

I nod; I've never been very talkative.

"Are you on your break? You work in the old folks' home?"

"No, I live here."

The driver doesn't understand, thinks I'm joking. Roused from my torpor, I walk away without further explanation, leaving him to draw whatever conclusions he pleases. I meet up with Bébel in his white jogging suit, struggling against the wind, mouth open, stopwatch in hand; his time today won't be so hot.

Yesterday I had a visit in my room from my wife, who brought divorce papers for me to sign. Our two children came with her. My wife's lover opted to stay outside. I was lying on my bed, and my children were at my side, looking at me as if I were ill. ("So how's school going?") Standing at the foot of the bed, looking around, my wife asked me if things were working out, meaning my room and the retirement home, my new life.

She'd changed, seemed more self-assured, and was wearing a fur coat. (The Billion has the same one.) I told myself that she must be happy. The children played an electronic game that made explosive noises. They stayed twenty minutes and then left. My wife thanked me for signing the papers. My children kissed me—just barely—on the cheek, the way you kiss old people.


Two attendants flank the residents assembled for the outing: "We're leaving now!" announces the one coming with us, who carries some stale bread for the deer. About fifty oldsters come lurching out of the Home, all dressed up, purses clamped under their arms and caps clamped down over their foreheads, equipped for the expedition. There's excitement in the air: We're taking the bus. Clarisse—who still puts on makeup every day, reasonably successfully—has gone all out for the occasion. Le Marec and Alice advance arm in arm, as on their wedding day, their heads nodding in tandem as if they were repeating *yes, yes, yes.* Bébel puts on a little burst of speed to sprint toward the head of the line, in case there won't be enough seats for everyone on the bus. I bring up the rear.

I go on all the outings. I took in the Lido nightclub show, Holiday on Ice, the Iggy Pop concert (not management's finest hour). I would never consider avoiding or flouting my responsibilities as a resident. I've chosen to live here, so I assume all the consequences and accept all the rules, including the outing to Thoiry. I feel it is my duty to take part, and I will not allow myself to weasel out of it. Group outings are part of the mortifying regimen I have decided to follow.

I sit at the back of the bus, not to make faces at people in cars, but to contemplate the two long rows of seats occupied by my companions, like a guard of honor for my humiliation. The attendant has sat down next to the driver, who glances at me in his rearview mirror while whispering in her ear, probably to get the lowdown on my story. The bus starts up: "We're off!" confirms an old lady in front of me, with a hint of anxiety in her voice and a look back at the Home falling away behind us. We leave the property and the adventure begins: the town, people, cars, the bustle of humanity. Safe behind the bus windows, the elderly passengers stare in astonishment at the spectacle of the streets. Vestiges of the past are pointed out for commentary: a grocery store, a monument, a facade; most of the time, everyone is quiet. We've left the town and now a fleeting landscape streams by, evoking voyages of long ago and ancient escapades like a scarred-over smile, stitched with wrinkles, that cracks open again: the Sunday picnics by the water; the trips to the seaside in Normandy; the walks in the forest of Fontainebleau.

After a while, moldering memories are no longer enough to pass the time, and the jaunt begins to drag on. Our passengers are getting antsy, wriggling on their seats; their bones ache, and they'd like to be home in bed. Clarisse undertakes to improve the mood: She claps her hands and intones, "Old MacDonald had a farm. . . ." A few residents join in, halfheartedly at first, murmuring more than singing; then, gradually, as the verses roll by, they perk up and soon the whole bus is chorusing, "E I E I O!" Myself included.

We arrive. The bus stops at the entrance to the park and the attendant gets out to present our reservations at the ticket office. A giant billboard shows life-sized animals: a tiger, a giraffe, monkeys, a rhinoceros. A sign warns visitors that they must not leave their vehicles or open their windows to feed the animals. The attendant loudly announces a precautionary pee-stop before we enter the preserve. In a mild panic, everyone prepares to leave the bus, looking around for animals; nothing in sight, all clear, quick, let's go pee. They crowd around the doors to the restrooms, on the alert; the coast is still clear, they wait their turns, the more they think about it, the more they need to go, hurry up, that's it, a door opens, at last. Oops, it's the men's side, Turkish style, the ladies have to squat down and there's nothing to hang on to, but so what, the tigers are on the prowl, the rhinos are charging, they'll pee standing up. They spatter the bottoms of their pantyhose, their shoes, there's no toilet paper, the giraffes are coming, the bus will leave without them, they don't wipe, just pull up their panties, ah!—the bus is still here. They get back on.

"Has everyone peed?" The safari can begin. The bus moves slowly along an asphalt road, on the lookout for animals. The preserve has been divided into different environments (a miniature savanna, broad stretches of water, ersatz jungle) to suit the various species in each area of the park. At the moment we don't see much except, off in the distance, some kind of disheveled ostrich with moth-eaten plumage, poking around with its beak, but now it's coming this way! The driver shifts into neutral. Clustering at the window, his elderly charges feverishly follow the progress of the bird, which dawdles with a haughty air, one movement at a time, one foot after the other, flexing its neck, surveying its surroundings with an arrogant eye. The ostrich circles the bus, peering up at the residents of Happy Days peering down, pressed up against their windows with surly expressions, craning stiff necks to see this strange sight ("You've never seen an ostrich before?"). Then the driver moves on: Giraffes have been sighted.

The giraffes hold our attention longer. Their majesty, their conviviality, and their supple grace allow everyone to admire their spotted coats and their rough tongues against the bus windows— which last remind Clarisse, incidentally, of a former lover who was endowed with an exceptional and quite talented tongue. Now we've stopped in front of the tigers' area; they've probably just eaten; a feline silhouette has been vaguely glimpsed through the foliage; Alice taps on the window ("Yoo-hoo!"); we leave them to their digestion. The elephant is asleep. The buffalo is lying low.

Monkeys are not shy. Monkeys are curious, monkeys are playful. The bus advances cautiously into the primate enclosure and soon a cheeky-looking band of macaques has surrounded the vehicle (ABS, television, air conditioning). They are clearly intrigued and, connoisseurs of automotive engineering, the first wave checks out the wheels, tackling the hubcaps, while the second wave tries to clamber up the sides of the bus, scratching the paint, climbing onto anything that juts out. One tries to unscrew a side-view mirror to admire itself at leisure, another brushes its teeth with a windshield wiper, while the rest hang obscenely from the windows, to the greater joy of the passengers, who reach out their hands. As we might have suspected, this reminds Clarisse of something: She rummages through her memories but can't put a face to all that fur, and that eager, almost clumsy impetuosity, not necessarily unpleasant, and those rather hair-raising manners. . . . "Marcel, at the Midsummer's Eve dance!" Up on the roof we hear scrabbling, like little mice, only heftier. Beginning to worry, the driver shifts into gear and gradually accelerates until we peel out of there on squealing tires, as monkeys bounce around in our wake like cheering spectators at an automobile rally.

We've completed the circuit. We get out of the bus for the tamer attractions, and our attendant distributes the stale bread intended for the does. I take my crust and head for the enclosure with Bébel. A depressed deer sidles morosely up to us and we stick our pieces of bread through the chain-link fence. The animal on one side and us on the other: each in his cage, his prison.

"What a life!"

"What'd you say?"

"Nothing, never mind."

That's as good as it gets. Whatever I do, I will always have this feeling of inexorable absurdity, this zoological, generic vision of humanity; like a ruthless entomologist, I will always turn this bug-pinning gaze on myself and my species. No, there isn't anything better. I'm where I ought to be, here, among those who no longer expect or wait for anything, abandoning themselves to a carica-ture of a life. Real life has become too cruelly human.

Around me, the old folks are nodding off, snoozing and slumping against one another. The landscape rolls past the windows. I stare straight ahead of me, sitting back in my seat, motionless, an elderly head leaning against each shoulder.

Sunday is usually visiting day. Relatives come to see the residents in the retirement home, to chat with them awhile in their rooms (you hear people shouting, "DO YOU NEED ANYTHING?"); sometimes they drag them off to noisy family gatherings, or take them for walks to tire them out. Bébel is expecting a visit from his children. He has traded in his jogging suit for striped pajamas and is staying in bed. His children pay part of his bill at the Home, and he always puts on a little show to justify his staying there. They've already tried taking turns having him live with them, an experience he definitely does not want to repeat. He's happy as he is and wouldn't leave his refuge for anything in the world. I greet him as I go by.

"Feeling fit today, Bébel?"

He waves feebly to me from his bed, at death's door.

"Ah, you're having visitors. Fine, see you later."

About once a month, I visit my grave. I'm still looking for a suitable epitaph that would sum up my life's work. The commemorative plaques stowed away in my closet are piling up like trophies; depending on my mood, I sometimes dig one out to reinstate it temporarily, before returning it to the closet. I let the front desk know that I'll be out that morning and I leave the Home on foot. I pass Jean walking silently in the garden, arm in arm with his daughter, endlessly retracing the path of the funeral cortege that carried off his beloved.

Outside, I run into Francis, a neighbor on our street, with whom I occasionally exchange a few words on the sidewalk. Francis has one passion in life: stock cars. He bought one at auction, a gem of a blue Renault 5 Turbo 2 that he polishes all week in his garage and takes out for a drive on Sunday, returning it afterward to its velvet-lined box. In overalls, bending over his pride and joy, Francis fiddles with something, cleans the engine with Q-Tips, and admires his handsome machine. Hands stained with grease, he holds out his forearm for me to shake. Together we gaze at the car for a moment, nodding in appreciation.

"You've got to admit, that's some car!"

"You know she belonged to Jean Ragnotti?"

I give him a look of amazement (I've never heard of Jean Ragnotti).

"And Bernard Darniche, is he still racing?"

"No, he quit a long time ago. He's in advertising, now. You up for a spin?"

"Thanks, but I'm off to the cemetery."

"Just a quick run around the block. . . ."

"No, really. Some other time!"

I clap Francis on the shoulder and go on my way. I would rather have been like him, living in ignorance and the here-and-now, with blinders on, instead of always having that panoramic view that grinds me into dust. I would have had a blue Renault 5 Turbo 2 that once belonged to Jean Ragnotti, and hands covered with axle grease. I would have zoomed around the block: vroom, vroom!

The cemetery is on the other side of town, not quite two miles away. Taking advantage of my outing, I stock up on cigarettes at the *tabac*; I wave in passing at Charbonneau Photo, where the owner waves blankly back to me through his shop window (*Who is that guy, anyway?*). Then I stop off at Ducasse & Son Memorials, where M. Ducasse, like his father before him (and unlike the photographer), is beginning to know me well.

"Bonjour, monsieur! How are you?"

"Still going strong, I must admit."

"You'll bury us all."

"Hey, if it were up to me. . . ."

"You've come to see your new plaque? It's ready. If you'll just come this way. . . ."

We go into the shed, where other personalized posthumous inscriptions and special orders are stored on metal shelves. *To our beloved grandmother Émilie; May your repose be sweet, as your heart was good; The memory of happy days comforts us in sorrow. . .* etc. I find the banality and indifference of other people's taste in funerary literature simply flabbergasting! Handing me a plaque of light gray marble that matches my headstone, M. Ducasse junior takes the liberty of saying, "If you want my opinion, this one is very nicely put." I check the inscription against the text I mailed in after my last cemetery visit, along with the usual technical specifications. I run a finger over the gilding, admire the engraving, and declare myself satisfied with the work. We then proceed to the office, where I pay my bill. "Thank you, sir. See you again soon!" And off I go, my plaque under my arm, like a salesman.

The cemetery is surrounded by a wall, an illusory rampart. I push open the entrance gate and advance slowly into the sanctuary of the dead. The stones welcome visitors with a silent lament; death mugs and robs the intruders; an army of crosses sights them in their crosshairs; the marble tablets tally their wounds; death calls the roll and digs another hole. I walk through the cemetery like an overdressed tourist visiting a nudist colony. The shameless tombs strip me with their eyes, seeing right through the flimsy fabric of my suit, dog-earing my simple page of life in the notebook of death. Even though I come regularly to the cemetery and have been preparing myself for a long time, I always feel uneasy among these orderly rows of tombs, this implacable architecture. One day, in my room, I took a tape measure and marked in inches a normal life span, eighty years, more or less, from which I subtracted thirty-five years, leaving forty-five still to go. Then, slowly, inch by inch, I rolled up the remaining forty-five years, until all I had left in my hands was a miserable scrap of ribbon as small as a fingernail: *When I'll be clinging to life by a single fingernail.* . . .

Standing beside my grave, once again I read my name and date of birth carved into the headstone. Just one more date, and everything will have been said. The cruel summary of a disarming truth I can't ignore. I replace my old epitaph with the new one. I contemplate my future resting place for a moment, shaking my head: "What a life!"

A physical therapist, the stimulating Dr. Roche, comes to Happy Days on Mondays and Thursdays to care for the old folks' rheumatism, rehabilitate convalescents, and help the more able-bodied among us keep in shape. One room, daringly called the Sports Room, has been fitted out with equipment selected by the therapist, and there he lavishes us with attention, which is directed for the moment toward firming up the gluteal muscles of a nurse on the rowing machine, while a little old lady calls for help on the parallel bars: "YES, YES, I HEAR YOU OVER THERE, THAT'S GREAT, KEEP GOING! Push with your legs, that's right, you're getting it—feel, they're already firmer. ALL RIGHT, I'M COMING, JUST A MINUTE—USE A LITTLE WILLPOWER!" Pedaling up his third mountain on the exercise bike, Chef is trying to strengthen his anal sphincter: "THAT'S IT, CHAMP, CLENCH YOUR BUTTOCKS!" Le Marec, on the barbells, goes after his personal record: "OKAY, MR. UNIVERSE, LET'S GET THOSE WEIGHTS UP IN THE AIR!" And in the background, techno music, to give the eardrums a workout. Hesitantly, I approach Dr. Roche.

"DON'T GIVE UP NOW, CHAMP! Yes, what can I do for you?"

"I've got a pain in the lumbar region, there."

"Do you work here at the Home?"

"No, I live here."

"Ah, so you're the gardener?"

"You could say that, yes."

"Lie down on the table."

I stretch out cautiously, and Dr. Roche lifts up my shirt to feel my back.

"You're going to do some abdominal exercises for me, we have to get some muscle tone in here, it's all soft. A good six-pack, and your problems are over! Let's put you in the captain's chair."

Meekly, I do as he says, and begin a series of leg

lifts. Next to me, Le Marec, exhausted, on the brink of tetany, grudgingly gives up.

"Well done, Mr. Universe. That's enough for today. We'll go for the record next time. COME ON, CHAMP! GIVE IT ANOTHER SHOT!"

After my workout, I stroll off to the lounge to enjoy the comfy armchairs. Gossip central, the lounge is sort of the Home's private club, where habitués gather around a pitcher of lemonade. At the residents' disposal is the lounge library, a collection of generously donated books saved from the shredder. Not many of the old folks read: The first page tends to put them to sleep, plus, it's all so futile, but, well, the books do look nice on the shelves. We tend to fall back on magazines instead—the love lives of the stars, the marriage of French crooner Michel Sardou, and Céline Dion's troubles getting pregnant. When Clarisse blurts out a way to get around that problem, Alice is outraged, Bébel sure wouldn't say no, and Clarisse cracks that'll be the day. When they ask what I think, I shrug. Bébel feels I'm being difficult: That photo of the singer in a clinging gown, her tummy totally flat—what more proof do you need? They move on to the next celebrity. I find them amusing, and forgive them. Any discussions

I might have on the outside would be more taxing for me, forcing me to cough up detailed opinions. As it happens, I have only a general opinion, which I express with a shrug and a vague little smile. I have often been taken for an idiot. That never bothered me, but I hated it when people tried to convince me of something or demanded that I explain myself. Here, at least, they leave me in peace.

Alzheimer died in the hospital. I'll never know his name. The poor soul couldn't even remember that.

I'm sitting on my bench. The grounds and garden are bright with lovely autumn sunshine. From his office window, the director of the Home studies me through the curtains. Even in high school, I used to sit on the steps in the courtyard for long hours, observing the comings and goings of other students. The principal watched me from his window. One day, unable to stand it anymore, he came to ask me what I was waiting for, sitting there, on those steps—and was I skipping any classes? Today, in the garden at Happy Days, I'm sitting in the sun, skipping life.

Jamel is cleaning the rooms. He's a nervous

little man, his white teeth chomping chewing gum, his eyes sparkling, a joke always on his lips: "Hi, Antoine! Guess what I'm doing!" And he pours water from his bucket onto the floor: "I propose a toast—to Happy Days. . . ." I smile politely and climb up on my bed to get out of his way. He swishes a mop swiftly around the floor, humming a popular tune, then stops at my bedside, propping himself up on the mop handle: "Got a question I'd like to ask you; it's been bugging me for ages. I just can't figure out what the hell you're doing here. You got something to hide, you screwed up, you lying low, you playing dead?" At that, I flash him a real smile: "Sort of." Jamel looks at me, stretched out on my bed, as though I were an enigma: "I'll never understand you." The cleaning man picks up his mop and bucket: "I'm off to do The Billion's room. I think she really likes me, you know, kind of like her son. Bye!" After Jamel leaves, I stay on the bed, waiting for the floor to dry.

In the afternoons, various workshops invite the residents to exercise their memories, or take a stab at the arts of pottery and painting on silk. Early on, I tried my hand at pottery, just to see, and sort of in memory of a friend who stuck himself off in the Pyrenees, where he became a potter! The activities coordinator began the class by installing each of us in front of a potter's wheel and a hunk of clay: "Today we're going to make a vase." Next came a demonstration of the basics, before an uneasy audience of oldsters: "Moisten the clay, like this; turn the wheel and use your hands to give your clay the desired shape; smooth it with your palms; hollow it out with your fingers . . . and you have a beautiful vase all ready to be fired. Now it's your turn!" Whereupon a hodge-podge of viscous vasiform objects ranging from banana peels through cowpats to dildos issued from the frantic fingers of the apprentices, who, brimming with good intentions, tried hard to get within striking distance of the idea of a vase—and failing that, you could always use it as an ashtray. I didn't last long, and now I decline to partici-pate in any workshops ("No, thanks, but no thanks."). Aside from the outings and shows organized by the management, I try to leave my days free, allowing myself only the bare min-imum of distractions from reality. A tour through the lounge, a walk through the grounds, back to my room: I kill time from day to day with the patience of a torturer.

\*    \*    \*

The municipal election campaign is in full swing. To include the residents in this civic debate, M. Révelli impartially assigns each mayoral candidate a day on the stump in our establishment. One after the other, the competitors take on the electorate of Happy Days, a potential harvest of a good hundred votes. Often, the visit consists of a swing through the rooms: two, three considerate words for each resident (without overdoing it, or you'd never get out again), a friendly pat delivered with some surreally optimistic encouragement, and the gift of a succinctly efficacious pamphlet (photo, candidate's name in large print) accompanied by luscious chocolate-covered bonbons—a giveaway somewhat neglected of late, due to budgetary constraints, and for those with high cholesterol, strictly forbidden. The pamphlets fill the maids' trash bags, while the boxes of chocolates fill the nurses' lockers, in anticipation of Christmas. The very best thing is to give a speech in the dining hall, with M. Révelli's permission, right before lunch, for example: a few minutes, no more, playing to the residents' avid attention, then reminding them of your name and wishing them "Bon appétit!" (with any luck, there might be something special on the menu that day). That's what François Le Gond decided to do, taking subtlety so far as to ring the bell himself in the courtyard: "Chow time!"

Equipped with a microphone connected to the dining-hall loudspeakers, François Le Gond replaces Richard Clayderman: "Is everyone here? Aha! I see a gentleman who hasn't yet reached his table. Let's hustle, shall we—there! Good!" François Le Gond introduces himself and immediately reassures his electorate that their lunch will be arriving in a few minutes, and in the meantime he will briefly present his platform, which comprises three essential points: "We'll skip the first two, they're somewhat technical, and frankly, no longer of much interest to people your age, isn't that right, you fortunate residents of the Happy Days! So, one essential point: A CLEAN TOWN!" In the larger sense and in every department: a big spring cleaning. François Le Gond then begins to stride up and down the checkerboard floor, tugging on the wire of his mike to navigate among the tables and string his listeners along. Forks in hand, the residents, not fooled for a minute, glare fiercely at the man snatching the bread from their mouths, unlike those mysterious "foreigners" he's busy accusing of this very crime. Meanwhile, caught up in his own enthusiasm, François Le Gond forgets all strategy and gets carried away, fences with an invisible opponent, slices the air, thrusts a menacing finger at the ceiling, stems the alien tide, tightens controls at the border. Groans of impatience, heretofore repressed, are heard from the residents: my cue to beat out a tempo for the revolt with my knife on my glass. My tablemates join me in delighted unison, soon inspiring the entire audience, now seething with outrage worthy of a prison dining-hall rebellion. The mayoral candidate finds himself obliged to wrap things up in a hurry: "I hear you! Bon appétit, my friends!" The waitresses immediately rush to serve the plats du jour, as a crestfallen François Le Gond leaves the premises amid the famished booing of the retirees.

During the meal, I observe my companions and think about that idiot Le Gond. What I like about these old folks is their focus on essential things and their fundamental, vital honesty. As if the proximity of death made all lies useless and required absolute sincerity, without any tricks or fakery.

LAURENT GRAFF

*   *   *

But things aren't always as simple and easy as I like
to think. Taking my morning walk through the
grounds, I find Bébel slumped on a bench, head
in hands, stricken by an unexpected despair.

"What's the matter, Bébel? Something
wrong?"

His wings broken, the jogger does not reply;
he's no longer in good shape, and his eternally
tanned cheeks are streaked with tears. I'm not
much good at comforting people, and psychology—
that ball-and-chain that holds man back and side-
tracks him from his true misfortune—is frankly
not my forte. After making sure he isn't ill—"You
want me to get a nurse?"—I sit down next to Bébel
and simply keep him company in silence. I'd best
keep quiet, or I'll only worsen my companion's
already-failing morale. While on my right Bébel
crumbles further into misery, however, I reflect
that there was always something about the old
man's obsessive exercise, now that I think back on
it, that was paradoxically unhealthy, or at least suspicious, and must have concealed some deeper
reality. Was it a way to repress the fear of death
or disguise some other distress? A kind of

44

screen, or armor? It doesn't matter: The fact is
that splendid Bébel has dropped his mask and is
sitting beside me in tears. To me this is one more
proof for the file of universal human unhappi-
ness, and I don't seek to learn any more about it.

Nor do I call Bébel back when he rises without
a word and heads for the street. I watch him go off
in his white jogging outfit and disappear through
the front gates of Happy Days.


It's afternoon, and Bébel still hasn't returned to
the Home. Informed of his absence by the nurses
on duty, M. Révelli questions his closest friends:
"And you, Antoine, did you notice anything?"
The director seems worried. And yet it isn't the
first time a resident has gone off on a toot, and
anyway, they're free to come and go as they please.
But Bébel's case seems definitely to upset him:
"Okay, then I'm going to tell his family." The
elderly runaway's children arrive late that afternoon, and after a short briefing, decide to go
looking for him without further delay. That's all
it takes to create a certain buzz in the residents'
ranks and start the rumors going. Driven—not
very honorably, I admit—by curiosity, I follow the

different developments of the affair, listening to what's being said in the halls and joining the discussions, which are going full steam. The family returns at nightfall, empty-handed. As a last resort, they decide with M. Révelli to call the police.

Given this turn of events, a committee meets after dinner in the lounge to consider the runaway's case. That's when Jean, breaking through his reserve, says timidly, in the midst of the wildest suppositions, that he thinks he knows where Bébel is. Everyone shuts up and waits for the rest. The whole thing goes back some twenty years. Without knowing him, Jean used to run into Bébel regularly, always in a bar, invariably drunk or well on the way. Until they met up again years later in the same retirement home, Jean remembered him as a wreck, a hopeless alcoholic, a raving drunk always getting himself thrown out of bars. Who would have believed it: The stubborn jogger was really struggling against slipping back into the abyss of drink. "Got to stay in shape!" That old devil! Now I understand—I knew there was something! In a way, it sets my mind at ease.

But I can't in all conscience let him slide.

Besides, all eyes are now on me. The consensus is that we ought to find him before the police do, and fix things up as best we can.

"Ah, it's you!"

"I've got a favor to ask you, Francis."

Flanked by Jean and Clarisse (who wasn't about to miss this), I'm standing at the front door of our local stock-car enthusiast. "I'm not disturbing you?" Francis had been watching the news on TV, a feature on the trials and tribulations of partisan politics.

"No. What's up?"

I quickly explain the situation, concluding with, "Can you help us find him? With a car, it would be easier."

He'll be ready in a moment, he just needs to change clothes and get the car out of the garage. It's a chance to put his Renault 5 Turbo 2 through its paces. Ensconced in my bucket seat, clinging to my safety belt, I watch the street shoot by like a horror film. The racing car's engine is roaring like an animal, and the bloodcurdling sound reminds Clarisse of—"Clarisse, please, not now!" As our designated driver, Francis sticks to his assigned objective, namely, hitting all the bars and getting Bébel back pronto before the police find him. The walls of the town are plastered with transient election posters; in our rush of speed, they overlap and blur, fighting to see which face will come out on top, and the winner is the grinning visage of François Le Gond, triumphing like a persistent subliminal image. On the sidewalks, the rare pedestrians whip past.

"What I think is, if we want to make sure we don't miss him, we ought to slow down a little, don't you agree? Maybe he's sleeping it off in some corner, in which case we might drive straight by without spotting him. Right, Francis?"

Huddled in the backseat, Clarisse and Jean admire a galactic landscape, streaked with shooting stars.

It's a big town and there are many watering holes still open at this hour. Fighting back nausea, I wobble into the bars, one by one, looking for Bébel. Stalwarts bellied up to the bar mutter soliloquies, reading the future in their beers; patrons sitting at the tables ramble through conversations about this and that, tiring out their tongues; wreaths of cigarette smoke drape themselves like B-girls around the necks of the smooth talkers. I ask the bartenders if they've seen an old man in a jogging suit, with a towel around his neck. They'd remember if they had, sorry, no. I say thank you, so long, escorted out by a drifting cloud of sweetish smoke. I get back in the car for another loop around the track: And they're off!

In the Café de la Pointe, fifth on the list, I've had it, I order a shot of rum and toss it back in one go, sighing with relief. *Where the hell has that asshole gone? I mean, we can't hit every last bar in town!* "Another, please! One for the road." Back in the car, I fasten my seat belt without a word, ignoring my companions' expectant expressions: "Well?"— "Just drive, will you!"

Two bars later, while we're passing a double-parked van, I suddenly glimpse a white jogging suit being mauled by three men who'd been putting up posters. Francis brakes hard and backs up to the scuffle, which indeed features our runaway jogger being ignominiously mugged. Without a second thought, Francis and I rush to rescue Bébel, shoving aside his attackers, who turn out to be rugby forwards. I regret forthwith not having tried to talk things over first, yet try nevertheless, a little belatedly, between two tackles, to begin a dialogue, but too haltingly and incoherently to be compelling. As for Francis, he's not faring any better, although he takes some pretty nifty evasive action in the face of a rather chunky adversary. We receive spirited and demonstrative encouragement from Clarisse and Jean, who have extricated themselves from the car through efforts nothing short of miraculous, and one could hardly ask more of them. When a police van on patrol happens along, four uniformed officers come out of nowhere, surrounding the belligerents and shouting, "Police!" The discipline of rugby players in the presence of referees is legendary; the melee breaks off, leaving me sprawled semiconscious on the playing field with a split lip.

Since we all wind up at the police station, you can't really say that the expedition was a sparkling success. I have recovered from my TKO and wait to be interrogated along with Francis and Bébel. In the neighboring cell, the three thugs have stuck smug smiles on their mugs, like that face they've been plastering all over town (considering that it's François Le Gond, I wouldn't feel so confident if I were they). As for Clarisse and Jean, they're busy answering Detective Namiech's questions in an office upstairs.

"Wait a minute! Let's back up a little, please. So, you left your retirement home with this guy Antoine to look for this guy Bébel, that's it? And Francis drove you around in a stock car?"

The two retirees confirm this, adding, "We checked out all the bars. See, you have to understand that Bébel. . . ."

Detective Namiech takes notes, writes down names: "But who's Chef? Is he the one who told you to tear down François Le Gond's posters?" This smacks of electoral manipulation (*Elderly Man Beaten by Goons; François Le Gond Disgraced*), the political scandal the young detective—who has seen all the gangster movies of Yves Boisset—has been longing to detect. Then his informants get to the dining-hall rebellion (with the policeman still writing away) and the boxes of chocolates: "Hold on, let's not get too far afield. Me, what I want to know is why you tore down those posters and who asked you to do that."

"But we didn't tear down anything! It was Bébel! He was drunk!"

Now it's my turn.

"Just a second. Okay, where do you live?"

"Well, to understand that, you'd have to begin at the beginning."

Finally, after three hours of grilling, a frustrated Detective Namiech gives up and lets everyone go. He never did get to the bottom of it.

The next morning, the nurses discover Bébel in bed, snoring like a buzz saw, and everything's back to normal. He insists that he simply treated himself to a little pub crawl; he needed a change of scenery, that's all. When his children phone him during the day, demanding to know where he was, what he did, he lies with a disconcerting naïveté that fails to allay any of their suspicions. The missing-person alert is canceled, Detective Namiech closes the file on the previous evening's events, and no one notices any connection between the two incidents. On the whole, we came out of it fairly well, and our heroes regale the lounge with the tale of their nocturnal adventure. Leaving Clarisse and Jean to recount their escapade, I withdraw discreetly to take a turn around the grounds.

*This earth with gentle step I trod; may I lie gently 'neath the sod.*

I've always loved benches. They're the image of a withdrawal, the seat of a contemplative distance, a peaceful marginality at the edge of the world. They represent a privileged observation post, a disengagement off the beaten path for those who know how to pause there. I've spent many an hour on benches taking stock of the world. Some of them are marvelous, unexpected, outlandish, and each site is a revelation. Someone sitting on a bench is detached from reality, or no longer belongs to it. This simple seat confers upon the sitter the status of poet, and lends a certain breadth of vision. If there is one place that ought to lie beyond the bounds of torment, it is the bench.

This is the first time I've laid eyes on her: She's sitting in the garden of Happy Days, wrapped in a coat that has become too big for her, and she's looking at the leafless trees. She must be a new resident, or else she is only revealing herself now, on this bench. I sit down next to her and share her contemplation. We stay like that, side by side, without speaking, united in a mutual presence that is subtle and pleasant. If she were younger, or if I were not wary of a religious interpretation, I would speak fearlessly of love to describe the inexpressible feeling that draws me to her at this moment, but I will speak instead of an intimate complicity, of the—accidental—collusion of minds that meet and reveal themselves to one another. This impalpable embrace lasts only as long as the breathing space our bodies will give us, so in that biting cold, it's not long before my neighbor shows signs of fatigue. Then I turn toward her, discovering her face.

"Shall we go back inside?"

Her name is Mireille and she arrived two days ago. Stricken with cancer, she has chosen to spend whatever time she has left far from any hospital. She's a *little old lady,* not special in any way, whom age and its alterations have reduced to a condition, an image, a cliché, as though she had never had a life "before," as though she had no history, no story of her own. Her wrinkles are not the mark of time, but a definite fact without past or future, aside from the looming death her situation implies. She is only what she seems today, frozen in old age, having no more future that would allow her to be seen in any other way.

Sitting at her bedside in her room, I decide to keep her company. Usually so aloof, so little inclined to sociability, I'm surprised to find myself chatting about nothing in particular, because although there was something ineffable and rare about our meeting in the garden, there's nothing exceptional about Mireille's conversation. The most I can say for her is that she's a bit less gaga than the other residents, with a more lively intelligence, perhaps, but she hasn't escaped that slippage, that natural deterioration that usually comes with age and inspires compassion. What leads me to remain at her side is not pity, however—I'm way too jaded for that. It's as if I were solemnly choosing her on this day, as an experiment, to help her and follow her until her death. Through her, I hope to understand the extinction of life.

Since my arrival here at Happy Days, I've already had close encounters with death (most recently with Alzheimer, for example), but in a much too abrupt and involuntary manner. Today I decide to accompany death—in the person of Mireille (if she accepts my presence), whom I met by chance in the garden—in its slow progress to its zenith. It isn't fear or anguish that imposes this choice, this conduct on me, but anger and incomprehension.

Seriously weakened by her illness, Mireille hardly ever leaves her room. She forces herself to take a short walk in the garden, weather permitting, and goes down to the dining hall whenever she feels strong enough. I accompany her during her long and difficult journeys, letting her hang on to my arm, matching my pace to hers. She considers me a friend and accepts my presence. She refuses to believe that I'm a resident of the Home and wishes to see in me a devoted nurse whose goodness extends even to self-sacrifice. Although perhaps she's trying to reassure herself about me. In any case, she appreciates my help.

In the same way, I'm beginning to like her; people are likable, when you get to know them. She tells me about her life, one existence among so many others: hers. I listen to her politely, feigning interest, when all I see in her story is the usual disheartening destiny common to us all. Sometimes I feel touched, the way one does by a close-up of a face in the middle of a battlefield; I may pay attention to an anecdote, before letting it melt away into the vastness of human history.

I become her confidant of the final hour, her private secretary, recording her memories and regrets. She's at that stage when life appears in its main lines, with scattered tiny details of over-whelming significance. She did what she could. Anyway, it's too late now.

She's lying on her bed and I'm watching her. Watching over her. When she has talked enough, she closes her eyes and drifts off into a premoni-tory sleep. I look at her as she sleeps, and wait in my chair for her to awaken.

\* \* \*

Christmas is coming. Frost ices the lawn with its fixative spray and covers the benches with gleaming lacquer. Bébel calls out to me as he goes by. Ever since his drinking spree, he hasn't been quite the same. He's lost some of his enthusiasm and splendor. Now he leaves his stopwatch at home and has shortened his exercise runs.

"These days, we don't see much of you anymore. It's true love, with your girlfriend!"

Could Bébel be jealous of the attention I pay Mireille? That's how I win a real place in my companions' hearts. Their friendship pleases me, but embarrasses me, bothers me. I want to be free of all ties, emotionally blank. And yet, love always remains a temptation, the only one left in spite of so much disillusionment. Perhaps the salvation of humanity lies in this inextinguishable desire, this stubborn belief in love. The coldest, most sorely tried of souls still cherishes the hope of loving again.

Before rejoining Mireille in her room, I detour through the lounge. Two deliverymen in overalls are putting up a Christmas tree as slender as a cypress in its packing net. Alice calls out an invitation.

"Come on, Antoine! We're going to decorate the tree!"

I go looking for Mireille to see if she wants to help. She's not feeling too tired, and accepts. It doesn't take much, sometimes. Give a big box of Christmas ornaments and garlands to some old folks, and you'll see their eyes shine with happiness.

"Antoine, catch!" Mireille tosses me the shepherd's star. Perched on a stepladder, I take charge of the upper branches. At the foot of the tree, my elderly companions unpack the box with delight. Clarisse has decked herself out in a garland and is playing the seductress, fanning the gentlemen with the end of her boa. Back from his jog, Bébel swats her on the derrière with his towel. Le Marec tries out his juggling skills, while Chef attempts to hoist up Jean so he can hang a crucial ornament. From my perch on high, I watch them having fun like kids.

Then I escort Mireille back to her room. This little interlude has done her good, and she kisses me on the cheek.

Every year, the management arranges for some entertainment on Christmas Eve. Last year, they hired a one-man band, who turned out to be a mite too raucous and enthusiastic. This year, M. Révelli is counting on a magician, one Dominique Zebb, to enliven the evening in a decorous fashion.

The tables in the dining hall have been arranged in a semicircle so that everyone can see the show, and space has been made beside the glass doors for the bedridden, who will be brought down when the moment arrives. The residents are invited to dress up for the occasion, and the hairdresser has done a sweep through the rooms earlier today. The staff have likewise been asked to make a small effort: Lipstick and glitter in the hair compensate for the resentment and vengeful mood of the nurses on duty.

Welcomed by M. Révelli, Dominique Zebb arrives toward the end of the afternoon to set up his props and special effects.

"Is that the famous box for sawing people in half?" asks the director. "But you don't have an assistant! You came alone? I thought magicians always had some ravishing young lady with them."

Dominique Zebb announces that he calls for volunteers from the audience—that's his personal touch.

"And those sawhorses there, what are they for?"

That is the linchpin of his show, a levitation number, his specialty. As proof, the magician directs a hypnotic stare at the director, who's getting worried.

"You know, aside from the staff, your audience will be entirely elderly people, most of them ill or invalids."

Just leave everything to Dominique Zebb, and in conclusion he passes his hands theatrically before M. Révelli's eyes. The director is beginning to regret his choice. Nothing's better than a good accordionist!

Handing her off to a nurse, I leave Mireille to get dressed and go to my room to do the same. I don't have an extensive wardrobe, no stylish finery, just the bare minimum. I do have a black tie for funerals; lacking anything better, I slip it on over a gray shirt—gray and black, they go together—worn with black trousers. I check in the mirror: I'll do. After a dab of cologne at my throat and under my arms, I go downstairs to the dining hall.

The corridor is thronged with residents; they've done their best to doll themselves up, and now they're eager to see what's on the menu and watch one of their number get sliced to pieces in Dominique Zebb's box. When I knock on Mireille's door, she greets me in an exaggeratedly elegant gown glittering with rhinestones; it's a little big on her, which makes her look like a girl trying on her mommy's dress. One day, Mireille opened her night-table drawer and brought out a family photo album: She showed me pictures of herself when she was young, her husband, her children, her grandchildren, an entire existence summed up in a few selected photographs, a kind of *This Is Your Life* that she consults now and then to cheer herself up. She was an attractive young woman, whom men must have looked at in the street and secretly desired. Today there's nothing left but an old lady, skin and bones, whom only an unavowed and despicable perversity renders desirable now and then in my guilty eyes.

With Mireille on my arm, I escort my date to the dining hall, where a good number of the residents have already gathered. It's a portrait gallery à la James Ensor, a riot of rouge, a permanent-wave contest, a fashion show of out-of-fashion styles on centenarian models. Sitting around the tables, the elderly revelers strike dignified poses in their party clothes for some hypothetical jury. Filled with the sense of ceremony demanded by the occasion, briefed beforehand by the nurses, they take care not to mess up their lipstick or wrinkle their shirts. They restrain their senile instincts and keep their buttocks clenched.

I sit down between Mireille and Bébel, who seems strangely untidy, rather under the weather. To tell the truth, his breath reeks of alcohol before the festivities have even begun and a single bottle has been uncorked. That old devil! In the center of the dining hall, getting ready to give a speech, M. Révelli waits for everyone to be seated. That's it, now we can get started. The director wishes us all a Merry Christmas and announces the program for the evening, introducing Dominique Zebb in his black cape; popeyed with enthusiasm, the magician casts spells on the residents, who squint at him distrustfully. Mindful of the "François Le Gond experience," M. Révelli invites the magician to withdraw in favor of the waitresses before things go to pot. At least the menu is traditional: That's something, anyway! Next year, it's definite: no more one-man bands or weirdo magicians. Accordion music!

Throughout the entire meal, Bébel ogles the wine bottle without daring to serve himself, while Mireille cuts up everything on her plate without eating even one morsel. I have been mistaken: Right up until the end, people will pretend, keeping up appearances and trying to hide behind them. Although the masks may crack at the approach of death, they never really fall. There will never be complete sincerity. People will always fight back, using whatever wiliness and lies life offers them. Until their last breaths, they'll try to set an absurd dignity against the approaching truth, which they'll refuse to believe and give in to, preferring to die clinging to a respectable pretense of life.

To accompany the Yule Log cake, the waitresses serve each resident a glass of champagne. Bébel feels authorized to drink, merely restraining himself from knocking it back in one gulp. Mireille wets her lips, affecting an air of exhilaration, then simply keeps holding her glass. That's when the first notes of Beethoven's Fifth Symphony blast the drowsy guests half out of their chairs, narrowly avoiding mass cardiac arrest. We're off to a good start. Dominique Zebb appears in the entrance to the dining hall, swathed in his cape, throwing lightning bolts (some kind of luminous firecrackers with blinding flashes). At a signal from the magician, the music stops abruptly and, with a wave of his arm, Dominique Zebb imposes silence on the crowd. Skeptical, the old folks keep a wary eye on the illusionist, adopting a wait-and-see policy. Standing behind the tables, next to the fire extinguisher, M. Révelli is on the alert, ready to intervene at the slightest screw-up. The magician advances slowly, his eye roving over the audience; then, flinging open his cape, he reveals the astounding outfit of a gladiator, or a lion tamer, with leather straps across his chest, a huge belt, and some kind of animal-skin underpants to conceal his privates. Openmouthed, the director thinks he's back at the Iggy Pop concert two years earlier (an unfortunate misunderstanding, due to a mix-up of dates, that brought on three fainting fits).

Dominique Zebb throws off his cape and performs a few simple tricks for his introduction, producing various objects: knives, sticks of dynamite, wire cutters, and more firecrackers—you name it. Then he moves on to the sawing-in-half number, brandishing long, flexible saws and scanning the audience in search of a guinea pig. I don't know what it is about me, maybe it's my absentminded expression, which people misinterpret, it irritates them, or maybe they just don't like my face, but ever since I was little, off at camp or in a subway car invaded by a bunch of juvenile delinquents from the projects, every time, I'm the one who winds up as the scapegoat. The magician points at me—"Who, me?"—and I stand, trapped and helpless, to walk around the tables, encouraged in passing by M. Révelli, who is visibly relieved. The residents applaud my theatrical début (hold on, don't get too carried away!). Giving me a quick hug, Dominique Zebb whispers some advice in my ear: "Just leave things to me, and you'll do fine." He has me get completely inside the box, discreetly points out the trick part (" 'Scuse me? Where is it?"), then closes the lid, a bit quickly for my taste. I hear the saws whistling above me; suddenly, I'm no longer completely satisfied with my latest epitaph; I promise myself to exercise more in the future, concentrating in particular on suppleness; and after all, when you think about it, life is beautiful!

It's magic! Happy to see the light again, I emerge from the box in one piece, to the bravos of the audience shouting my name. I humbly thank my public and prepare to return to my seat, but Dominique Zebb places a hand on my shoulder: "I'm not through with you yet." And he points to the sawhorses.

\*    \*    \*

New Year's Eve is quieter, more intimate; few residents last until midnight, and, well, this celebration of the passage of time is sort of depressing. A year comes to a close: You hesitate to say "one more" or "one less"; a new year begins. . . . Will you make it to the end?

Time goes by relentlessly, indifferent to the suffering of those it sweeps off toward certain death. Feeling weaker and weaker, Mireille gradually sinks into gloomy melancholy. Lying on her bed, in a mournful torpor, she contemplates me coldly, as if encroaching death were glaring at me defiantly through her eyes. I try to meet the challenge, to endure her look without flinching or losing my resolve. In those moments, Mireille is already gone, and nothing—no word, no smile—can bring her back to life. I must simply wait until a reflex in some mysterious depths returns the dwindling gleam of life to her eyes. So I no longer leave her side: Step by step, I follow the tenacious, methodical, laborious progress of death at work. Mireille now seems to have grasped my motivation and my growing interest in her. She isn't shocked or offended, however. She accepts my presence at her side and goes along with the experiment without protest.

From now on, she'll have all her meals in her room. I have a tray sent up to me and eat with her so that I can keep my eye on her. I leave only when the nurse on duty is attending to her or helping her bathe and dress. During such times, I take a short stroll through the grounds before returning to her bedside. I'm behaving like a true voyeur, peeking through the keyhole at what's going on behind the door, trying to spy on the slightest movement on the other side. I want to be there when the door slams shut on her.

It snowed last night. Mireille's room is flooded with pure light. She's sitting up in bed, a pillow wedged behind her back. She has barely touched the breakfast sitting on the rolling bed-table; a drop of café au lait on the edge of the cup and a missing corner of toast show that in spite of everything, she did try. She greets me with a sly little smile: *Don't worry, you didn't miss anything.* I wish her good morning, then go to the window to contemplate the garden beneath the snow.

"Close the curtains, will you? It's a lovely day to die, don't you think?"

That's when I catch sight of Bébel's white jogging suit swinging gently beneath a tree. He has hanged himself with his towel, wearing his stopwatch around his neck and a skullcap of snow on his head.

*Don't worry, you didn't miss anything.*

As irony would have it, Bébel is buried facing me, meaning in the grave across from mine. Out of curiosity, I went to his funeral, passing myself off as a friend, which I was, if you like. Relegated to the second row, behind the family, I watched the burial from my tomb. I experienced the ceremony rather as a foretaste of my own obsequies (to within a few yards), with family and friends besides. I wonder who will come to my funeral. It doesn't matter.

I'll be accused of cruelty and cynicism, reproached for my lack of feelings and humanity; no one will understand the pain and effort my project has cost me, and the necessity that drives me on. For this mortifying cynicism is not an end in itself, but a necessary evil in my attempt to fathom what lurks behind our miserable human condition, an anesthesia that allows me to perform open-heart surgery on man and rummage through his guts. Searching for the human in humankind. Only the callous, indifferent attitude of a surgeon can give me the freedom and distance indispensable to my insane quest. Of which I am, by the way, the first victim. I offer myself as a human specimen, sacrificing my own life for the good of a generic global vision. My retirement in Happy Days should allow me to understand what an individual's life is, stripped of all diversions, seen in the light of its dénouement. For the moment, I still haven't discovered anything (in the sense of discovering a buried treasure) that would give this life some tolerable deeper meaning. My idea of humankind is probably pitched too high for that, or else I'm stubbornly ascribing to humanity qualities it does not possess.

\*     \*     \*

Bébel's suicide this January has cast a pall over the Home. People are astonished, they don't understand, and they turn away, perplexed. Those who know, or think they know, say nothing. "It" can't explain everything—the trouble ran deeper than that. And suddenly, they feel they know what was troubling Bébel, they feel inexplicably, dangerously close to him. Quickly, they turn aside, they seek amusement elsewhere, to forget.

Tonight is movie night at Happy Days. Once a month, management hires a projectionist and shows a recent film. Not very knowledgeable in such matters and hoping to avoid any bum choices, M. Révelli leaves the selection of these movies to his only son, a seventeen-year-old movie buff with discriminating albeit perhaps somewhat apocalyptic tastes. We've been treated to *Man Bites Dog* (a faux documentary about a serial killer), David Cronenberg's *Crash,* Lars von Trier's *The Idiots,* and many more. The audience is rather sparse, but we do get the occasional cry of horror during the shows, and once we even had to interrupt the projection to evacuate a spectator, which testifies to the depth of emotion aroused by a film when it's truly well done. M. Révelli, alas, is too busy to attend these showings, but he has every confidence in his son, who intends, with the unconditional support of his father, to pursue a promising cinematic career, we can be sure of that.

Today the film is *Blood Red*. There's a knock on Mireille's door, and Clarisse pokes her head into the room, more to find out what I could possibly be "up to" with my "sweetheart," really, than to invite me to the movie (or perhaps she'd like to take what she thinks is Mireille's place). Replying that I'd rather stay with my "sweetie," I decline the invitation; Clarisse nods with a malicious smile and disappears.

"You're a vulture."

I turn toward Mireille. She's staring at me icily. She says it again.

"A vulture."

So, I try to explain my motives to her, calmly, as simply and delicately as possible, assuring her, moreover, of my sincere affection. She seems to understand. Looking out the window, she makes me a proposition. She's going to die soon: She feels it, she knows it. She will allow me to stay with her if I grant her one request. The final wish of a dying woman, a last-minute extravagance, a stunning coup before the coup de grâce. I'm all ears.

That very evening, I ring Francis's doorbell.

"I have a favor to ask of you."

"Oh, yeah?" The racing enthusiast is wary. The last time I asked a favor of him, we wound up at the police station. "Another old guy has flown the coop?"

I'm not sure how to broach the subject. "It's a ticklish situation. It's Mireille. Actually, I'll need your car. For a few days."

"And to do what?"

"To take her on a trip. You see, she's going to die soon, and she'd like to visit the seashore one last time."

Francis gets a dreamy look in his eyes. "The sea?"

"Yes. Well, I mean, the waves, the open water, the salt air, you know—the sea!"

"For how long?"

"Depends. It's hard to say. In my opinion, she's on her last legs. A week, maybe."

"Have you ever driven this kind of car?"

It's settled. Francis agrees. He lets me in and gives me the car's registration papers.

"Be careful! Bring my car back to me in one piece! I'm counting on you!"

"Yes, sure, don't worry."

"No funny business!"

I follow Francis into the garage and he shows me a few things I need to know, explains some tricky points. "You got all that? Here, take the keys."

I thank him, take his hand in both of mine and shake it warmly: "I'll repay you someday." (I'm not sure how, but, whatever.) A visibly nervous Francis walks alongside his car as I drive slowly just down the street to Happy Days, where I park in front of the entrance gate.

Mireille is waiting for me in her room. I've packed her travel bag with some clothes, her makeup kit, and a few mementos she insists on taking with her. I help her dress and pick her up to carry her. I check to see that no one's loitering in the hallway. . . . The coast is clear: Let's go. Mireille clings to me, her arms around my neck, feather-light. No one sees me as I make a break for it, shouldering open doors, and soon I'm hurrying along a path in the middle of the night, carrying my escaping Cinderella to her getaway-pumpkin. I settle Mireille in the front passenger seat and buckle her into her seat belt, while Francis adjusts the straps to fit her snugly. Then I go fetch our bags. *What the hell am I doing?*

It's too late to turn back now: I shift into first— "Gently!" calls Francis from the curb—and I'm off, heading for Normandy, with an old lady at death's door, in the car of Jean Ragnotti, stock-car driver.

I haven't driven for a long time, haven't even touched a steering wheel since I came to Happy Days. ("All right, Francis, relax, I got it!") How do you turn off these fucking headlights? I'm a little rusty at this.

We drive through the night in silence (so to speak), dazed by the engine racket of the Renault 5 Turbo 2. No question, Jean Ragnotti's car runs like a dream! Even if Mireille and I wanted to exchange a few words, I'd never hear the quavering voice of my passenger over the din of the motor and I'd have to scream to ask her to repeat herself, besides which she's hard of hearing ("What did you say?").

Anyway, what could we talk about? Words are vain and paltry things, ringing hollow in the huge void that engulfs us just as this highway does as we barrel along. In the face of death, what could we say that wouldn't betray our weakness? Only silence has something honorable and courageous about it. Speech shows up our insignificance so much it's pathetic, and almost ridiculous.

I remember taking a trip in a hearse; it was for the funeral of my wife's—my ex-wife's—mother. Every car in the procession was full, so I rode all the way to the cemetery, in Brittany, with the employees of the funeral home. Dressed in their sober suits, they'd squeezed over on the one seat of the hearse to make a little room for me. For the first hour of the trip they were extremely serious and respectful. Then, as the miles went by, their conversation began to loosen up, and soon they were speaking freely, paying no attention to my presence anymore. They chatted about this and that, including the racy stuff men talk about among themselves, as you can imagine. I watched the landscape slipping by, as my mother-in-law lay behind me in her oaken coffin. This incongruous juxtaposition of life and death simply confirmed me in my take on existence.

In our racing hearse, Mireille and I speed toward the sea. Why has she chosen the sea? Perhaps she wants its vastness to establish some link between herself and the infinite? The sea imposes modesty, instills humility. She needs this last enlightenment, this encouragement, to resign herself to death without regret.

A stock car sure goes through a full tank in a hurry! For the second time, I pull in at a gas station. Seizing her chance, Mireille announces that she'd like to pee. I park in a handicapped space and carry her to the restrooms. Hearing the sound of flushing inside, I hesitate to enter the ladies' room, but in the end we go inside. A young woman in a suit is freshening her makeup at the sink; I smile at her, showing her my burden to justify my intrusion. She nods in understanding and watches me in the mirror between brushstrokes. I set Mireille down in front of a toilet stall and wait at the door, idly studying the ceiling. That woman's taking an awful long time with her makeup. . . .

"Are you all right, Mireille? Yoo-hoo!"

That's when an entire busload of boisterous tourists returning from a Céline Dion concert hits the gas station. A dozen ladies, their bladders bursting, pile merrily into the restroom, warbling one of the trying-desperately-to-get-pregnant

Québécois star's songs: *I searched for your soul / From pole to pole / I used all my charms / To keep you in my arms.*

"Mireille? You okay in there?"

Emerging at last, Mireille answers my question: "I used my visit to make the big deposit. Traveling agrees with me, apparently."

That's the spirit!

We reach Ouistreham in misty weather to find the town deserted in the early-morning hours. Following Mireille's directions ("It's over there. . . ."), I take the beach road and we drive along the shore looking for the Hôtel Bellevue. Mireille stayed there on a vacation, forty years ago. Memories: "It's a charming little hotel, with flowered balconies and white shutters." So we're hunting for geraniums, in the middle of winter, at five in the morning, in a fog so thick you could cut it, and aside from that, everything's fine.

"There was also a little garden in front, with a windmill."

"Don't you want to wait until daylight, Mireille? And anyway, it's too early to get a room, at the Hôtel Bellevue or anywhere else."

I park in the lot at the casino, facing the sea,

and turn out the headlights. Through the open window ("You could crack the window a bit please, Antoine, to let the smoke out. Thank you.") we can hear the waves, like a distant murmur ("Could you put out your cigarette, Antoine? It's chilly. Thanks so much.") that would have sent us into a gentle reverie, Mireille and me, and we could have dozed off, delightfully soothed by the rustling of the water, and gotten a bit of rest, for example.

"Aren't you tired, Mireille?"

"No, not at all. I'm telling you, the trip is doing me good."

I shoot a sidelong and slightly suspicious glance at Mireille.

Six o'clock. "Whenever we felt like it, my husband and I, we'd take a ferry over to England. The dock must be someplace over there."

I tell Mireille I'm going to step outside for a cigarette. I start laughing to myself, though. Sometimes life can be so comically insane and absurd! I'm pacing up and down the parking lot of the casino at Ouistreham smoking a cigarette; in a few hours, I'll get a hotel room with an old lady; I'm driving a stock car; my name is Antoine; I'm thirty-six years old; the sun's about to come up; the wind's blowing through my hair; the Earth orbits around the Sun; the universe is infinite; six billion human beings; it's noon in New Delhi; I stamp out my cigarette in the parking lot of the casino at Ouistreham, in Normandy, France. How do you find your bearings in that nesting set of matryoshka dolls? What place does a person have in that vast ensemble? What can he aspire to? Is every individual destined to be just a trifling elementary particle—a conscious one, alas—condemned to a measly little life?

Sitting on my bench in the garden at Happy Days, however, I do sometimes feel that I attain a certain form of liberation, of "superexistence," that surpasses ordinary renunciation and frees me from all ties and encumbrances. It's like a soothing weightlessness at a motionless point, a kind of existential levitation that suspends the normal course of life. You have to go both as far from and as close to yourself as possible, undoing the attachments that bind you to the world and letting go of all life lines. Then nothing has any hold on you anymore, and you sail above the world, borne along by a new wind.

\* \* \*

The Hôtel Bellevue no longer exists.

"Oh, that's been gone for a long time! It's condos now."

Disappointed, Mireille sulks in her bucket seat.

"Don't worry. We'll find another hotel. Look, this one here seems quite nice." I pull up in front of the entrance and ask Mireille to wait in the car while I go ask at the front desk about a room.

"Double or single?"

"Double, double." I fill out the form in my name (profession: retired), and the receptionist— on duty since rosy-fingered dawn, a little bit groggy, but charming all the same—hands me the key and invites me to have breakfast in the hotel, then corrects herself after consulting her watch: "That is, in a half an hour from now."

In the meantime, I carry Mireille to the room, one floor up, and install her on one of the two beds separated by a night table, with a bedside lamp to be shared or fought over.

"This place isn't in the same class as the Hôtel Bellevue. Now, that was something!" I head downstairs for the bags. "Ask them to send up my breakfast, Antoine."

I've always been against euthanasia, believing that we owe it to ourselves to live out our allotted time, even in unbearable suffering. But going down the stairs, which were somewhat steep and rather dangerous for anyone with their arms full, for example, I reflected that, in certain cases, euthanasia would be understandable, it all depends. Taking the worst-case scenario, moreover, prison can be an enriching experience, just like a retirement home.

Mireille seems to be forgetting that we're here for her to die, quickly, if possible: Francis is waiting for me to return his car. I give her ten days, after which, willy-nilly, we're going back to Happy Days. Enough is enough! I'm perfectly prepared to be nice, if that can make things easier (I hate complications), but my patience is limited!

"Excuse me—would it be possible to have breakfast in the room?"

In this season, the hotel is practically empty. In the hall I passed a couple on the verge of breaking up; they'd come here to the seaside to revitalize their relationship, but as far as I could tell, the marine atmosphere was not having the desired effect—far from it. Perhaps they ought to try the mountains, some scenic precipices?

While having a cigarette downstairs, I also noticed a writer sitting at a dining-room table by a window, hard at work, his head in his hands, staring at a blank sheet of paper and wondering what important thing he might possibly find to say in his attempt to revolutionize the French novel. I have no advice for him, but if I were he, I wouldn't take it all too seriously and would try to lighten up a bit. Unless the quarreling couple have separate rooms or the writer is sleeping in the cellar, that makes a total of three rooms occupied out of the hotel's twenty. Assuming that the squabblers don't throw furniture around and that the artistic soul doesn't wail at night, it should be peaceful here. Any upset would more likely come from Mireille and her rebellious deathbed whims.

For the moment, I more or less succeed in getting her to stay in her room by ordering her to rest, to stay lying down, in the hope that she'll never get up again. She insists that she feels fine, accuses me of keeping her imprisoned, of wanting to bury her alive, and threatens to lodge a complaint. I do my best to remain calm and avoid confrontation, then I go back downstairs for another smoke. Just how much shit have I gotten myself into? Whatever made me bring her to Normandy? So that's the situation.

And now Mireille starts wriggling around, propped up on her arms as if to get out of bed: She demands that I take her outside right now, or she'll call for help. Preparing to carry out her threat immediately, she takes a deep breath to let out a scream while I manage to stop her in extremis.

"Fine, we'll go out! Calm down. Shush!" Holding a finger to my lips and the other hand out toward her mouth, I tiptoe over to Mireille, who's stuck in apnea—throat closed, eyes rolled back—and beginning to turn blue. "Mireille?" Forgetting all my gloomy vows, I thump on her back to get her breathing again, I thump harder and harder, until a prolonged rattle—a surprising sort of pectoral fart distinctly different from a belch—escapes from her open mouth with sound effects reminiscent of diarrhea. Amazing. Her lungs cleared, Mireille gradually recovers, while I keep patting her back and observing her progress, not without a certain curiosity. But the fit has passed; there's nothing to see anymore. That was a close call! I decide to take her to the beach in a warm coat for some fresh air.

I'd have felt terrible if she'd died under those conditions, trying to yell for help; on the other hand, it would have been rather beautiful and revealing. But one always dies lousily, absurdly. One always leaves behind the unsolved "mystery of life," without ever coming up with a satisfying or even encouraging justification for having lived, aside from the perpetuation of both the species and the aforementioned mystery. A faint and cruel consolation. We must resign ourselves, for want of something better, and in the hope that a hypothetical messiah will appear among us to enlighten us with luminous words. But wherever could this messiah come from?

The sea. It's lovely. The waves, the sound of the waves, the horizon.

Sitting on a dune, Mireille and I contemplate the open water. On the beach, a windsurfer prepares to challenge the elements, slipping into a wet suit that covers him from head to toe. I've always wondered what pleasure anyone gets from this kind of activity; once, in my distant youth, I tried my hand at climbing, and once was enough for me. It should be clear by now that I am not a

man of action. All my life, so to speak, I will have
devoted myself to an abstentionist contemplation
verging on absence. It's the only way I've found to
avoid compromising myself too much with ordinary reality. I've tried to penetrate to the heart of
things, insofar as there might be one; I have set
myself up as an observer to try to grasp a destiny,
glimpse a path, a perspective, beyond what is
given us to see. But I am forced to acknowledge
that I do not have the talent of Moses; the sea
does not open before me, and the horizon still
remains blurry, distant, and closed to me, even as
the windsurfer now hurls himself out to meet it,
riding the waves full speed ahead. . . . Good luck!
I don't expect a miracle, just a little breach to
explore, a reason for hope, a glimmer of salvation, something to aim for and something to fall
back on. Three dimensions cannot contain my
dreams and my ideas of grandeur.

Huddled against my shoulder, Mireille clings
to my arm. No matter what she says, she no
longer has the strength even to look at the sea,
so painful is the spectacle of the world that will
go on without her. She needs support, but even
so, she doesn't give in and still strives to pit herself against life, with my help, and claim her

share, tiny though it may be. She clutches my arm as if it were the last handhold before a plunge into the abyss. She digs in her nails, as if to leave her mark there, the sign of her passage, an indelible tattoo, a vaccination against oblivion. I can't give her a new lease on life, so I let her borrow my body, and give her my skin for parchment. I'll carry her signature on my flesh, since the human heart can't be trusted. Long after the wound has healed, there will still be a scar; can one say that as surely about the wounds of the soul? At this moment, on this sand dune, Mireille is contemplating all the vanity and inadequacy of life, the pitiful progeny of the human race. Then she takes from her pocket a comforting snapshot of her grandchildren. After staring at it coldly, she suddenly breaks into a smile as her eyes fill with tears. At this moment, on this sand dune, Mireille is contemplating all the tenderness and discreet charm of life, the touching nature of the human race.

What are Mireille's tears? Simple drops of water in an ocean of sorrow. Yet they contain the special salt that adds a bit of human flavor and thereby gives savor to life. Whatever I think of it, without that humanity—imperfect, and flimsy, and ridiculed though it may be—we definitely wouldn't be worth anyone's while.


I take Mireille in my arms—alley-oop!—and we return to the car. We drive at random along the coast, in silence. Out on the beach, a lone teenaged boy is putting a kite through its paces; the souvenir shops are closed for a spell of winter amnesia; scattered snowflakes look for a place to land. It's the dead season.

"I want some oysters."

I check my watch—four o'clock—and pretend I didn't hear.

"I want some oysters!"

You'd think she was pregnant! Let's not get all worked up about it. I explain to Mireille that right at this moment, it would be difficult; but, if she wants, this evening we could go to a restaurant to eat as many oysters as she likes, and who knows, maybe they're on the hotel menu, in which case we wouldn't even have to go out—I mean, you know, hunting for them. Mireille shoots me a disdainful look: "Party pooper!" I've somewhat lost the habit of living with someone and must admit that it's not easy getting back into the swing of it. I glance over at Mireille's door, after confirming that my passenger is not wearing her seat belt (my oversight), then check out a plane tree a hundred yards ahead, in a perfect spot, right on a turn, but I remember Francis's concern about his car.

"Mireille, you don't know how lucky you are!" She hasn't a clue what I mean and shrugs snootily as we whiz silently past a fish store.

"I've got some periwinkles, if you like."

I take stock of the fishmonger's display: A few kinds of tortured-to-death fish lie on their bed of ice; a tied-up crab is agonizing under a wad of seaweed; some mussels that just can't keep closed anymore are beginning to confess; and in the bucket the fishmonger holds out to me, a handful of boiled winkles desperately await my helping hand.

"Fishing isn't always a piece of cake, you know."

I know. "Okay, I'll take the winkles." Although I'm not sure that Mireille will prove as understanding.

Back in the car, I give Mireille the sack of winkles, which she weighs in her hand in amazement, like a Mafia bagman just handed a fistful of small change: "These aren't oysters!"

Brilliant! There's no use explaining to her that the fishing business isn't exactly booming these days, why waste my breath; I drive straight ahead, eyes on the road. At the first grumpy word, I'll throw her out through the windshield.

"And how am I supposed to get them out of these tiny shells? With my little finger?"

Francis is an organized man who plans ahead and leaves nothing to chance. His car toolbox is a veritable gold mine, of course, containing everything you might need for repairs (the usual tools—screwdrivers, wrenches and the like), but also a whole bunch of tiny pointed utensils, including a collection of sewing needles stuck in a strip of leather in order of increasing size, perfect for winkling winkles from their shells, as it happens. And just by chance, in the course of driving around glumly but gamely, I've pulled over at the edge of a cliff by the sea, at the end of a coast road, with a solitary bench for a guardrail and an invitation to relax. After selecting my needle from the toolbox, I close the car trunk and grab Mireille and her bag of winkles without saying boo. Rather jolted about by our rally run, she doesn't let out a peep, allowing herself to be carted off, still shaking. I put her down on the bench and hand her the needle (*Here, now eat up!*). Then I stand there before the panorama, bearing witness to the wideness of the world, going so far as to address it with informal familiarity: *Can you tell me what the fuck I'm doing here?!*

I've already spoken of my fondness for benches, and for one moment I'm tempted to treat Mireille to a big dose of bench, to ditch her there with her winkles, like a grandmother forgotten by the edge of the road in August. But watching her stabbing away at her shells on her bench, with snowflakes in her hair, beyond pitiful, I can't help suddenly feeling real tenderness, true love. Mireille abruptly appears to me in all her innocence and strength, the saving image of humanity, of a naïve, almost infantile simplicity. Obviously, and I know this now, I never would have abandoned her (I would have turned around), regardless of any moral obligation. For the first time, I hold someone's life in my hands, almost literally, and that life, frail though it might be, is worth more than anything. On this cliff, I measure its full weight, stripped of every

LAURENT GRAFF

blemish, placed in the balance against death, and
I tip the scales irresistibly in life's favor.

When Mireille has finished her bag of winkles,
and tossed the last shell over her shoulder, I
crouch in front of her and take her thin knees in
my hands.

"I'm such a burden. . . . Aren't you tired of
dragging me around?"

Smiling at her, I shake my head. "Let's go back
to the hotel."


Mireille died last night, in her bed. A good way to
go, they say.

I went down to the front desk; the couple were
settling their bill, each paying half, already
arguing about the divorce proceedings; at his
table, the writer seemed to have found an
opening and was plunging forward frenetically.
I was careful not to shock the receptionist:
"Excuse me, would you call the police for me,
please?" The police asked me a few questions,
and I gave them the phone number of The
Happy Days.

Standing at the foot of the bed, I contemplate
Mireille's body in the company of her son. A

nice guy, serious, levelheaded. After I'd explained things to him, he assured me that there wouldn't be any complaint lodged about kidnapping, he'd see to that. I thanked him. He doesn't seem too broken up: "It was only to be expected. We'd been preparing ourselves for this." I feel like replying that for my part, I've been preparing myself for almost twenty years now. But this is neither the time nor the place to tell my life story and expound my personal outlook on things. Besides which, given the circumstances, I'm not sure he would understand. I don't want to risk having him change his mind and decide, after reflection, to file a complaint, not for kidnapping anymore, but for incitement to suicide, or even for murder. At his request, I describe Mireille's last days, skipping the details and rough spots of a difficult cohabitation. And so he ends up thanking me in turn for helping his mother carry out her last wishes. Don't mention it. Somewhat at a loss, he asks my advice about how to deal with the authorities and the funeral home, never suspecting that he stands before an expert.

"She's beautiful, don't you think so?"

I reply that maybe it's because she died in her

sleep that she seems so serene, so peaceful. He nods. I think he likes me.

He insists that I go with him to city hall, then on to the funeral home recommended to us by the clerk, right around the corner on a neighboring street. I take charge of the arrangements to transport the body, offer my opinion on the selection of the coffin ("You think so? It's a bit plain. . . . Shouldn't she have something more elegant?"). We dine together at the hotel restaurant. We order oysters. He's in computers. I tell him that I'm the gardener at Happy Days.

*All my life, I've let myself die.*

The grounds and garden are bright with lovely summer sunshine. In the large shady spots beneath the leafy trees, little groups gather to play secret games or weave plots they dare not disclose. Watched by counselors, the other children play dodgeball, tag, ring-around-the-rosy. A few loners, ill at ease, watch their comrades at a distance or look glum off in a corner, cultivating a promising originality. Sitting on my bench, a straw hat shading my eyes, my cane in hand, I contemplate the unchanging spectacle of life. And I still ask myself the same questions.

At the end of the path stands the Home, somewhat changed, altered to suit the requirements of its new vocation. At the front gate, it says: THE HAPPY DAYS VACATION AND RECREATION CENTER.

Aside from a little rheumatism, I'm as sound as a bell. Ten years ago, M. Révelli's grandson took over the management of Happy Days from his father. The Home had been in a bad way after a few unfortunate accidents, no longer enjoying its former high reputation in the area, so the new director decided to turn things completely around by making the place a children's holiday camp and daycare center. I was worried about what would happen to me, but M. Révelli (the grandson), whom I'd watched grow up, reassured me immediately: I'd been there so long I'd become part of the place, in a way, and I'd be staying on as the "gardener" no matter what happened. And so here I am, sitting on my bench, surrounded by children!

A boy comes over to me. He hesitates, then finally sits down at my right.

"Monsieur, where do you live?"

I ask him his name.
"Alain."
"May I call you Al?"
"Okay, but where do you live?"
"I'm coming to that, Al, I'm coming to that."

## About the Author

**Laurent Graff** was born in 1968. Archivist, widower, and father of two children, he lives on the outskirts of Paris. *Happy Days*, his first novel to be published in English, was awarded the Prix Millepages 2002.